"Everyone is unique, and different, and special! So perhaps there are times when we don't see eye to eye with someone, or just could not understand another person. That is normal and what's important is that we work out our differences and accept others for who they are!"

Big Bird

My Buddy, Forever
by Heather Durenberger
illustrated by Anastasia Honcharenko

To David Paul and Lucas, my heart is so happy that you've found lifelong friendship. May we all learn from you and the example you've set of how to include others. I love you both dearly and am so very grateful to be along for the ride.

To all our Minnetonka teachers and staff, I extend my heartfelt gratitude for your dedicated service to the next generation and our community. For those who planted seeds of belonging in our boys, we're grateful for lessons that bring endless joys. With your guidance, love, and kindness, so true, they've found friendship, enduring and anew.

Many years ago, in an outdoor kindergarten class,
Met two boys, unsure, across the green grass.
Lucas, his smile wide as the sky's brilliant hue,
And David, uncertain, with eyes curious and true.

David, never seeing someone like Lucas before,
Thought, "What's different here? I think I'll explore."
With Lucas's laughter, like sunshine's warming ray,
They giggled and laughed and started to play.

Their teacher, wise and gentle, seized the chance,
To nurture a friendship with a knowing glance.
With patience and grace, she wove a thread,
Binding their hearts, as she graciously led.

David learned Lucas had Down Syndrome, no less,
His momma assured him, there's no need to stress.
She said, sweetie, everyone is different you see,
That's what makes us unique, you, me, and he.

A playdate was planned, they played basketball and snacked,
They shared laughter, found joy, and never looked back.
With each passing moment, David's doubts did fade,
For in Lucas, he found a new buddy he'd made.

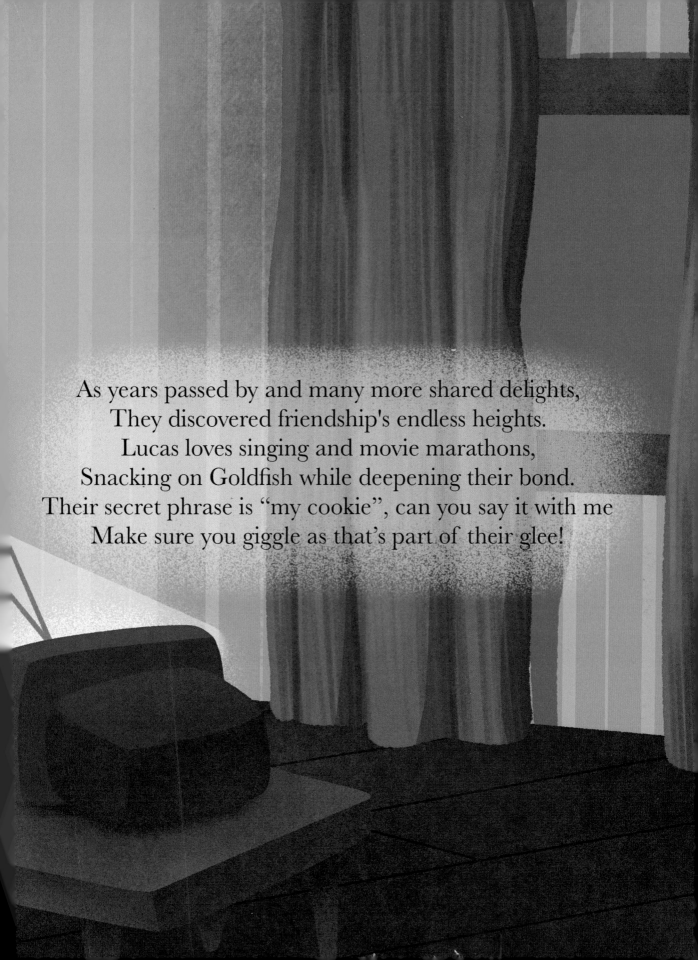

As years passed by and many more shared delights,
They discovered friendship's endless heights.
Lucas loves singing and movie marathons,
Snacking on Goldfish while deepening their bond.
Their secret phrase is "my cookie", can you say it with me
Make sure you giggle as that's part of their glee!

As David and Lucas went through the school years,
They remained in classes together, they were truly peers.
From baseball games to burgers they'd share,
Bowling and cookies, adventures beyond compare

There is a gift here for you and me,
I wonder if it's something we might see.
To embrace each other without fear or doubt,
And cherish the bond that's built throughout.
With empathy and kindness, we'll go far,
For in our differences, lies our brightest star.

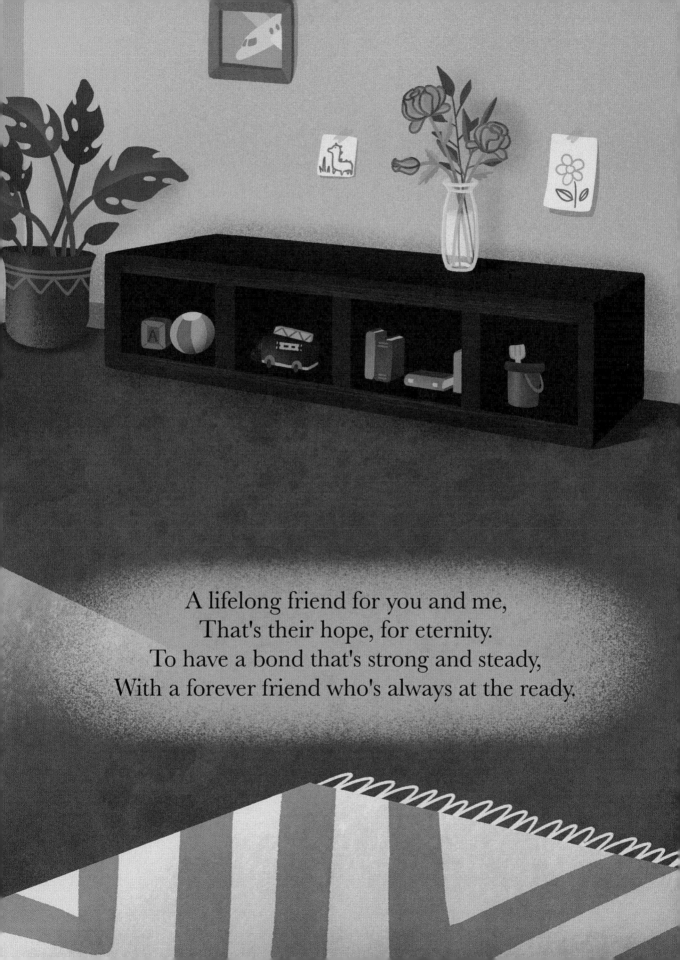

A lifelong friend for you and me,
That's their hope, for eternity.
To have a bond that's strong and steady,
With a forever friend who's always at the ready.

David and Lucas' wish for you,
It is to enjoy the gift of friendship, forever true.
To sharing life's journey and creating memories together.
Oh what a ride it's been with my buddy forever!

Discussion prompts for young readers:

In the story, David, a young boy, learns about differences. What do you think makes someone different from you?

When David felt unsure about Lucas, he talked with his teacher and his mom: Who can you speak with about people different from you?

Lucas and David find they have much in common, such as a love of basketball and watching movies. What interests do we share with others, and how do things we have in common help connect us?

Lucas's teacher ensured all the kids were having fun during recess. How can we ensure that all kids, including those with disabilities, can participate in the games and fun?

David and Lucas played baseball and went bowling together. What are some games everyone can play together?

Sometimes, people with disabilities might need extra help. How can we show kindness and offer help without making them feel uncomfortable?

Can you recall a time when you extended a helping hand and brought joy to someone's life?

As we learn from David and Lucas, such value is found in including others and being kind. What will you do today to include others?

Made in the USA
Monee, IL
24 November 2024

71119302R00017